MEGA MASH-UP

Trolls vs. Cowboys
in the Arctic

Nikalas Catlow
Tim Wesson

Draw
your own
adventure!

nosy crow™

An imprint of Candlewick Press

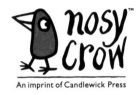

An imprint of Candlewick Press

Copyright © 2012 by Nikalas Catlow and Tim Wesson

All rights reserved. No part of this book may be reproduced, transmitted, or stored in an information retrieval system in any form or by any means, graphic, electronic, or mechanical, including photocopying, taping, and recording, without prior written permission from the publisher.

First U.S. edition 2012

ISBN 978-0-7636-6271-4

12 13 14 15 16 17 BVG 10 9 8 7 6 5 4 3 2 1

Printed in Berryville, VA, U.S.A.

This book was typeset in Agenda.
The illustrations were created digitally.

Nosy Crow
an imprint of
Candlewick Press
99 Dover Street
Somerville, Massachusetts 02144

www.nosycrow.com
www.candlewick.com

This book needs

YOU!

What if some cool Cowboys

and some hairy **TROLLS** wanted to get RICH?
What if they went digging for GOLD
in the Arctic?
What if the ice started to CRACK
and they all **FLOATED OUT TO SEA?**

Would they SINK without a trace?
Or would they come up with
a CLEVER PLAN?

You'll have to finish the illustrations
and find out....
Prepare to **LAUGH**
while you doodle
and SNICKER while
you read.

Your hand

INTRODUCING the TROLLS of Duff City!

Pong

Drudge

Gruff

Bogella

Bonehead

Introducing the Cowboys of Duff City!

Texas Tom

Lasso Larry

The Sheriff

Hi-Ho Sylvia

Billy Two-Hats

You'll need these....

DRAWING tools

These are the **3** tools that Nikalas and Tim used to create the artwork in this book.

felt-tip pen or marker

pencil

crayon

PEN

crayon

Using different tools helps create great drawings.

texture page

pen zigzags

crayon rubbing from linoleum floor

pencil cross-hatching

crayon rubbing from wood floor

pencil rubbing from wooden door

scribbly pencil

There are lots of ways you can add texture to your artwork. Here are a few examples.

pencil dashes

crayon rubbing from wall

pen circles

DRAWING TIP! Turn to the back of the book for ideas on stuff you might want to draw in this adventure.

Chapter 1
The Fools' Gold Rush!

Draw a
snowball
above the Trolls.

On a cold Arctic day, some hairy Trolls are caught in a **bLizzaRD**. "Let's take shelter in that cave," says Gruff, the leader of the pack, brushing snow from his beard.

Add a hungry polar bear.

Add some more Trolls.

The Trolls huddle together for warmth. Suddenly, Bonehead holds up a shiny rock. "**Look at this!**" He tests it with his teeth. CRUNCH! "It's GOLD!" he yelps. "Ow!"

Yuck! What have the Trolls been eating?

The Trolls make plans to build A MINING TOWN. "First things first," says Bogella, Gruff's **Stunning** wife. "We need a **Salon** so we can keep our beards looking nice and a **Saloon** so we can spend our riches on French fries and snow cones."

Gruff is thinking about the saloon.

Add a Troll peering through the window.

But news travels fast, and just as Pong is giving Gruff his first **beaRD tRiM**, a bunch of Cowboys turn up. "YEE-HAW!" cries Texas Tom. "We heard there was gold in them there icebergs. We've come to stake our claim!"

What's piled on the wagon?

"We were here first," says Gruff. "This is our town, and the gold is ours." The Cowboys laugh. "Call this a town? You ain't even built a mine. Step aside, **fuzz-face**." The Cowboys get to work, and in no time at all, the ice shelf is home to Duff City.

Grr!

HAIRY HOTEL SALOON

Turn this building into a jailhouse.

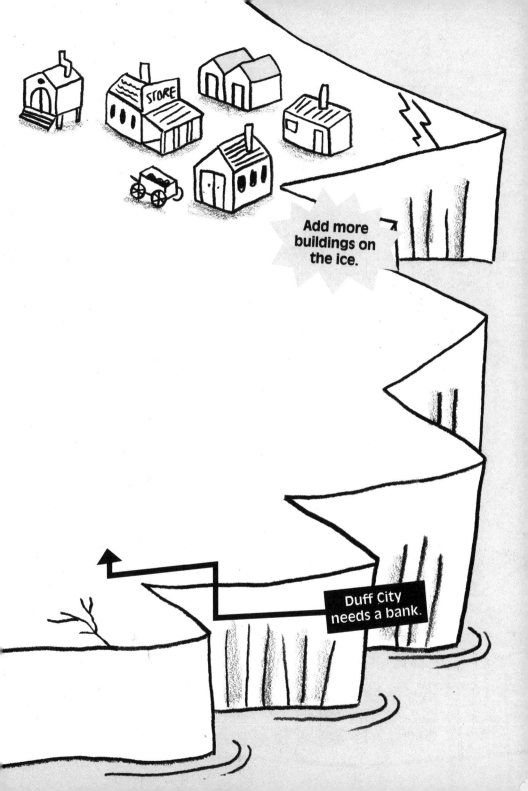

Add more buildings on the ice.

Duff City needs a bank.

Draw Texas Tom flying out the swing doors.

Draw in a flea-bitten old dog.

Mining for gold is thirsty work, so the Cowboys and Trolls spend many an evening in the saloon. Soon, **tempers** start to fray. "What do you mean, my wife ain't no lady?" snarls Gruff, throwing Texas Tom through the saloon doors.

Hi-Ho Sylvia runs the town's store. "What you guys need is the **GOLD-TECH-DeLUX-5000**. It sniffs out gold at fifty paces, but I've only got the one in stock—"

"Mine! It's mine!" cries Bonehead.

"Hand it over, you **thieving TROLL!**" snarls Lasso Jack.

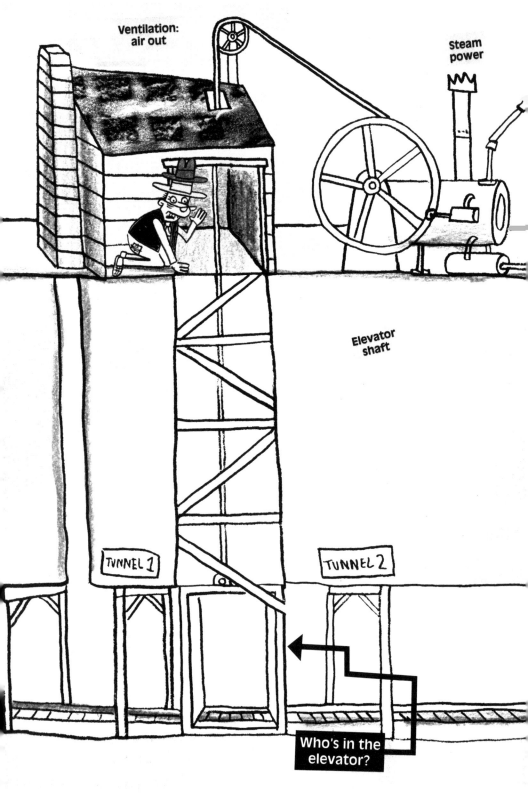

Billy sprints back to the **SALOON** with the good news. "THE FELLAS HAVE STRUCK GOLD!"

Chapter 2
Duff
City
Adrift

The Trolls and the Cowboys **STAMPEDE** toward the mine. Then . . .

1.

You write the scene!

2.

3.

4.

SNAP

What's buried in the ground?

Add more debris!

CRASH! The impact of the falling elevator has caused a CRACK to appear in the ice, which zigzags quickly across the mine floor. But the Cowboys and Trolls don't notice. They're too busy rubbing their sore heads.

Add a battered Cowboy hat.

OUCH! What hit Bonehead in the eye?

Add a mining cart.

The Trolls form a tower, and the Cowboys **CLAMBER** up it to reach the surface, using the Trolls' beards as handholds.
"Ow!" cries Drudge, rubbing his chin.

Add minerals and rocky texture.

They all stagger back to DUFF CITY.
"Er, guys, we're breaking away from the mainland,"
says Bonehead.

But his words are drowned out by an almighty cracking.

Finish the crack!

CRACK

Half the Hairy Hotel is left on the mainland, and half travels away with them on the ice shelf. "I guess that means we'll only get half as many customers now," remarks Gruff.

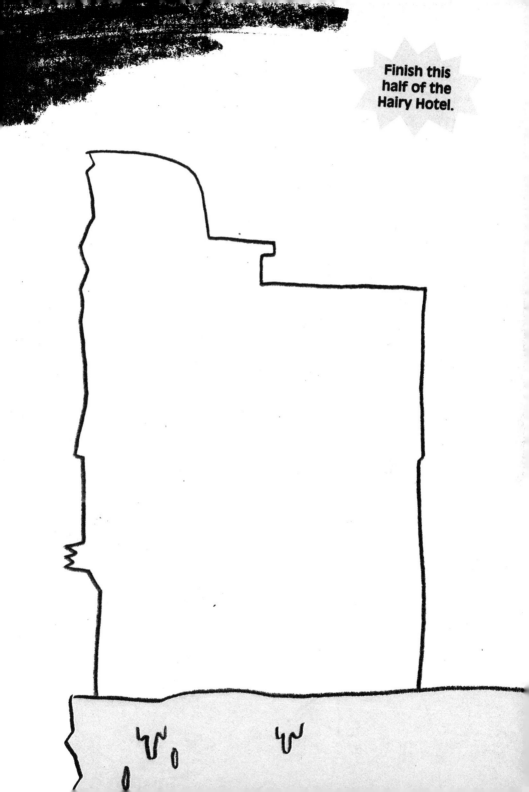

Finish this half of the Hairy Hotel.

A fight soon breaks out, and the Sheriff does his best to break it up. "Boys!" he cries. "Don't make me throw you all in **JaiL**." He looks around. "Actually, where is the jail?"

Who is Lasso Jack lassoing?

They stare at the jailhouse as it sinks into the sea.
The hot sun is **MELTING** the ice shelf,
and it's getting smaller, and smaller. . . .

Draw the jail sinking into the water below.

Chapter 3
Anything You Can Build, We Can Build Better!

"We need a plan to get out of here before we're all **fiSH fooD**," says the Sheriff. "Think, boys, think!"

The Cowboys frown and stroke their chins.

The Trolls fiddle with their beards and look stumped.

Make the Cowboys look thoughtful.

Make the Trolls look confused.

"GOT IT!" cries Billy Two-Hats. "We build us a boat and get the **HECK** off this ice! What you got, Trolls?"

Looks like Billy has a good idea.

"Well, that's embarrassing!" mutters Pong, while
Billy Two-Hats can't stop laughing.
Just then, a passing seagull **POOPS** on Bonehead.
"That gives me a great idea!" cries Pong.

After a frenzy of work, the Cowboys unveil their **PADDLE STEAMER** and celebrate by shooting wildly into the air and whooping.

Add a flag.

Finish the paddle steamer.

"Oops," says Hi-Ho Sylvia. "That seagull's had its last poop, all right."

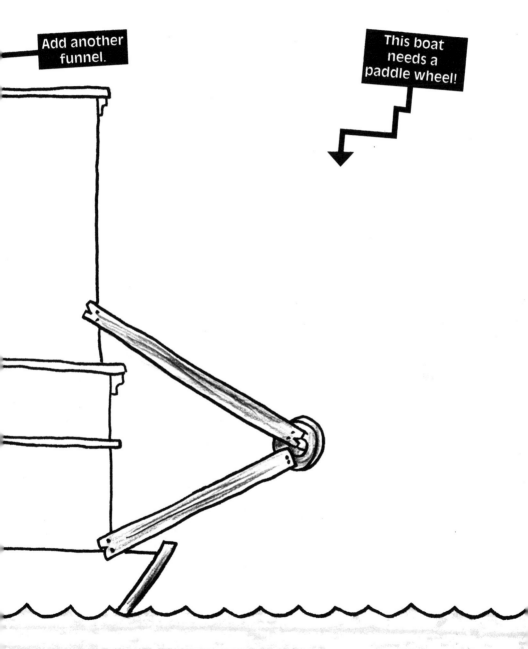

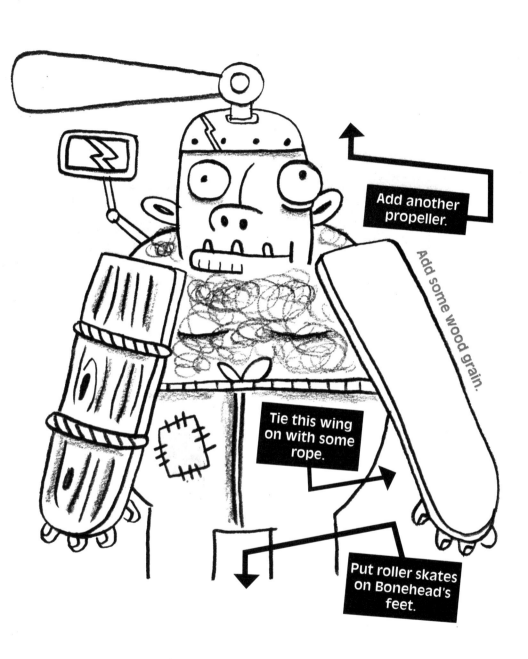

The Trolls have been busy, too. They reveal the Trollicopter, complete with **SNOW RAMP** from which to launch it. "Look and learn, boys, look and learn," Grudge declares confidently. Bonehead takes a run up, flapping his arms crazily . . .

Help Grudge build a ramp for the Trollicopter.

and crashes straight into the Cowboys' paddle steamer. "You IDIOT!" cries Texas Tom. "OUR CHANCES OF ESCAPE ARE SCUPPERED!"

Finish the crash!

Chapter 4
A Troll in a Bottle

The rumpus wakes a nearby hibernating walrus.
Not pleased, he starts to **LUMBER** over in
their direction. . . .

The walrus roars in fury.
"H-H-H-He looks pretty m-m-mad!" stammers Billy.

In desperation, Lasso Larry throws a CAN OF BEANS
at it, followed by a bottle of SODA.
The walrus swallows them both! **BURRP**!

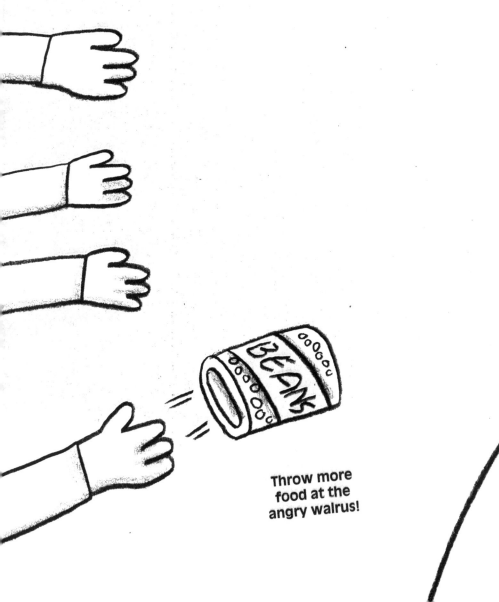

**Throw more
food at the
angry walrus!**

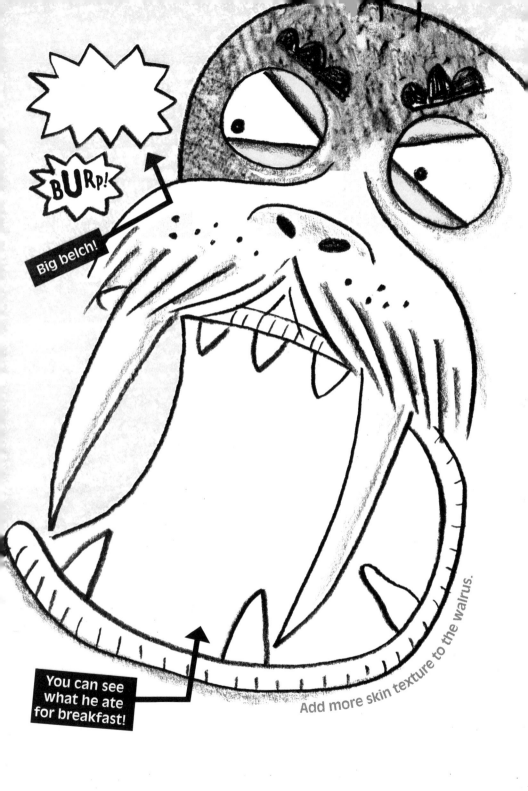

The walrus grabs Bonehead and stuffs him into an empty soda bottle. "Ha!" it says, taking a mighty swing and **throwing** the bottle MILES OUT TO SEA.

Add more skin texture to the walrus.

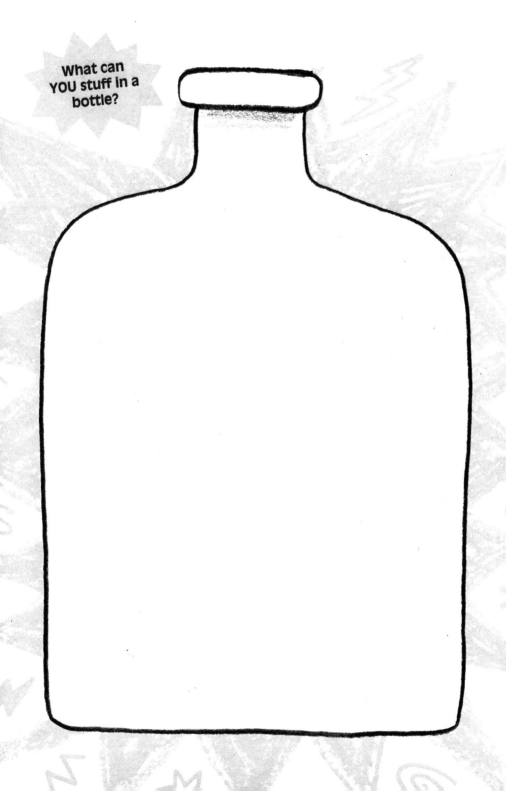

What can YOU stuff in a bottle?

Meanwhile, ONE THOUSAND MILES AWAY on a sun-baked shore, Tony Vegas, the billionaire and theme-park owner, is designing the **RoLLeR coaSteR** of his dreams.

Suddenly, something hard bounces off his head and splashes into the pool.

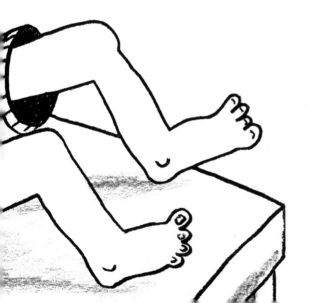

Add a fancy swimming pool.

Tony Vegas frees Bonehead and listens
in AMAZEMENT to his story.

Then Tony has a brilliant idea. . . .
"Come on, Bonehead!" he cries. "**THERE'S NO time to waste**! Now, where did I put my speedboat keys?"

OOH! What's Tony found at the back of the drawer?

Add wood texture to Tony's drawers.

Chapter 5
If You Build It, They Will Come

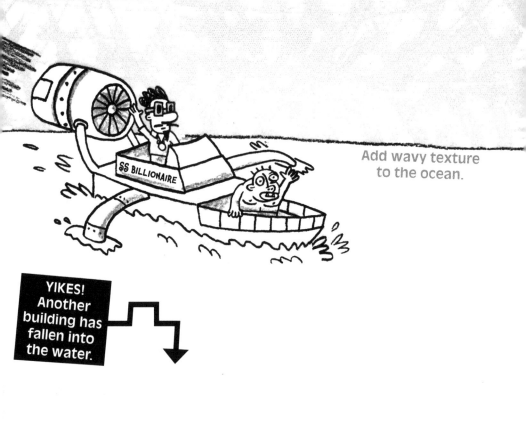

Add wavy texture to the ocean.

YIKES! Another building has fallen into the water.

By now, Duff City's iceberg is tiny.
Everyone is watching nervously as the sharks circle,
GRINNING HUNGRILY. Suddenly they see something
speeding toward them on the horizon. . . .

LOOK! A meerkat in a dinghy.

Tony Vegas swooshes up in his speedboat.
"We can't come any closer, or we'll scratch my lovely
paint job," he says. "You'll have to swim
across." **THE SHARKS LICK THEIR LIPS**.

YIKES!
The water is full
of sharks and
polar bears!

"I don't THINK so," says Pong. "Trolls, start SHAVING!"
"Sylvia, get KNITTING!" hollers Billy Two-Hats.
"We're gonna lasso a lift to shore! YEE-HAW!"

We need more hair! Draw yourself as a hairy Troll.

Soon Lasso Jack is whirling a large **HAiRY LASSO** around his head and WHOOPING. Gruff rolls his eyes. "Just get on with it!" he cries. Jack takes his shot and catches the bow of the **SS BILLiONAiRE**. "Hold on tight, y'all. . . ."

Lasso the boat, and don't touch the sharks.

Draw the
lassoed
SS *Billionaire*,
and watch the
paint job!

Fill the water with tiny boats.

"WHEEEEEEEEEEE!" cries Billy Two-Hats, clinging on for dear life as the iceberg is towed back to land. A **flotilla** of boats has gathered to greet them.

Safely on shore, TONY VEGAS shares his vision with the Cowboys and the Trolls. **"AN ARCTIC GOLD RUSH THEME PARK!"** he exclaims. "It's going to be mega!"

OOH! Finish Tony's grand plan.

Chapter 6
Walking in a Winter Frontier Land

Arctic-o-matic snow and ice generators are set up on the ice shelf, and they begin scooping up seawater, extracting the salt, and turning it into snow. The ice shelf grows and grows, and soon **CONSTRUCTION** of the theme park begins.

Design an ice generator.

Who's watching on the beach?

It's Opening Day, and the line of customers is **STRETCHING as far as the eye can see.** Business will be booming!

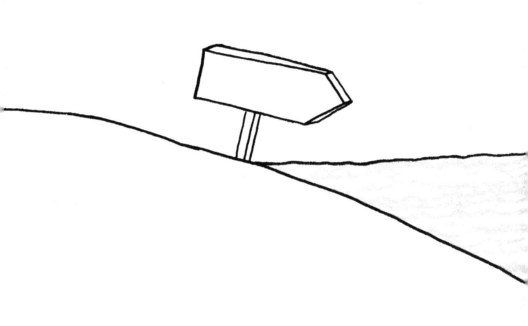

Add a line
of eager
customers!

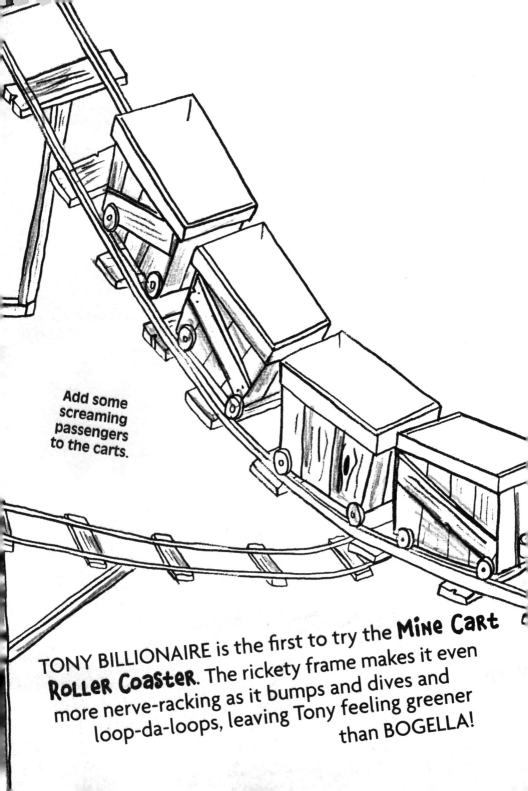

Add some screaming passengers to the carts.

TONY BILLIONAIRE is the first to try the **Mine Cart Roller Coaster**. The rickety frame makes it even more nerve-racking as it bumps and dives and loop-da-loops, leaving Tony feeling greener than BOGELLA!

The Sheriff and Bonehead are selling refreshments and souvenirs. "Get yer ARCTIC GOLD RUSH T-shirt here!" cries the Sheriff. "Print your own design for a fiver!" Mystifyingly, Bonehead's slurpy slug **SNOW CONES** are proving less popular.

Design your own T-shirt.

Gruff is working on the Bridge of Trolls and loving it. A family of goats wisely gives this one a **Pass**.

Add a goat running away on the bridge.

The theme park is a **ROARING SUCCESS**! The Cowboys and the Trolls toast their newfound riches with mugs of hot chocolate and watch the **FIREWORKS**

light up the night sky. "That was one rootin' tootin' adventure, all right!" declares Billy Two-Hats.

WOW! Create an amazing fireworks display!

"I got **Stuffed** into a bottle by an angry walrus,"
Bonehead says, reminiscing. "We turned our
ice shelf into a theme park," adds Texas Tom.

"Thanks to Tony Vegas," adds the Sheriff.
"But we never did find any GOLD," says Gruff.
"Gold?" cries Billy Two-Hats excitedly. "Where?"

Picture Glossary

If you get stuck or need ideas, then use these pages for reference.

Things you might see in Duff City

STORE

General Store

Stagecoach

Wagon

A Goat on the Run

Products from the General Store

If you like, you can copy the pictures. OR you can draw your own versions.

BEANS

SPAM

JAM

DANGER THIN ICE

A Danger Sign

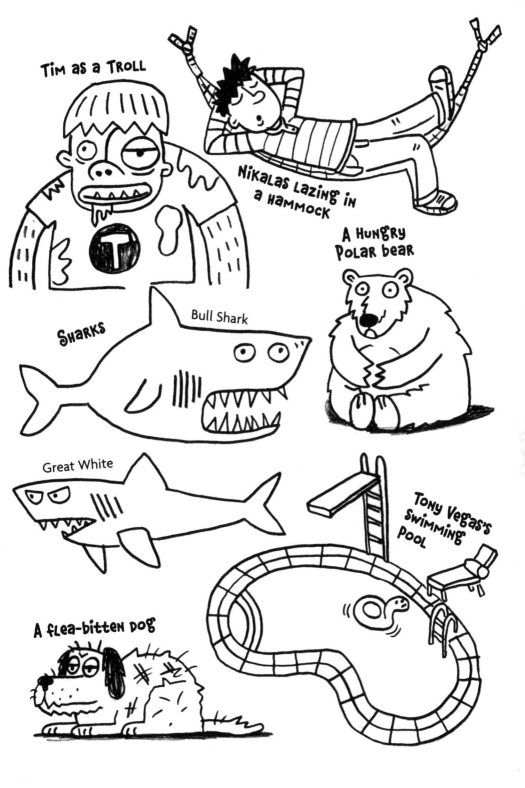

Tim as a TROLL

Nikalas Lazing in a Hammock

A Hungry Polar bear

Sharks

Bull Shark

Great White

Tony Vegas's Swimming Pool

A flea-bitten Dog

More Picture Glossary

Here are some more ideas.

Silk Underpants

Things in Tony Vegas's Drawer

Self-Portrait

Spare Shades

Hair Tonic

Gold Mirror

Blingy Ring

Spare Comb

CRACK

Sound Effects

Cowboy Snowman

A TROLL brain

If you like, you can copy the pictures. OR you can draw your own versions.

Visit our **awesome** website and get involved!

Website

www.megamash-up.com
Upload artwork and get the latest news.